No Ponies in
the House!

Do you love ponies? Be a Pony Pal!

PONY PALS

No Ponies in
the House!

Jeanne Betancourt

Illustrated by Richard Jones

A
LITTLE APPLE
PAPERBACK

SCHOLASTIC INC.
New York   Toronto   London   Auckland   Sydney
Mexico City   New Delhi   Hong Kong   Buenos Aires

Thank you to Amy Nadeau for sharing her
love and knowledge of small pets.

ISBN 0-439-42627-8

12 11 10 9 8 7 6 5 4 3 2 1   3 4 5 6 7 8/0

Printed in the U.S.A.   40
First printing, March 2003

Contents

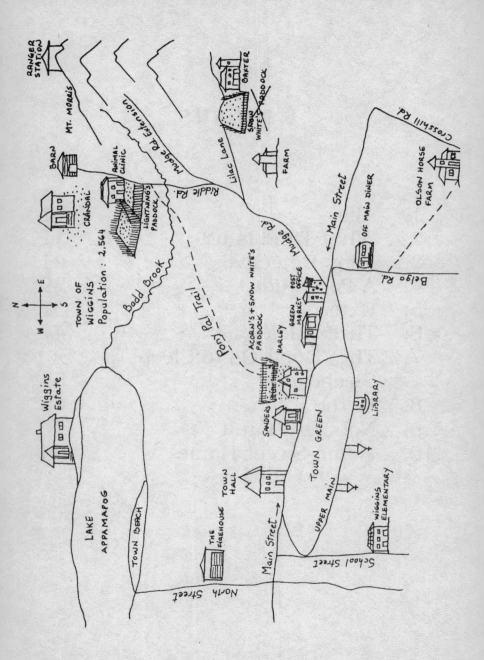

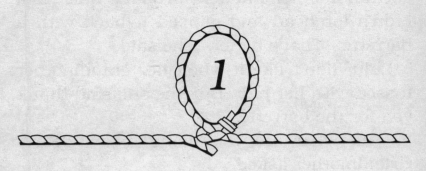

Alfie

Lulu Sanders ate breakfast and looked out at the paddock. Her pony, Snow White, was at the fence. Anna Harley's Shetland pony, Acorn, stood near the walk-in shed.

As soon as I finish my cereal I'll feed them, thought Lulu.

Lulu's grandmother poured herself another cup of coffee. "I'm going up front," she announced. "My first client will be here soon." Grandmother Sanders had a hair salon in her house. She would be busy all day cutting, curling, and blow-drying hair.

Grandmother Sanders brushed hair from Lulu's forehead and clipped it back with a barrette. "That's better," she said.

Lulu didn't like it when her grandmother fussed with her hair. But she still said thank you for the barrette.

"And what are you doing today, dear?" Grandmother asked.

"Snow White and I are going over to Pam's," answered Lulu. "But first I have to feed the ponies and clean the paddock."

"Animals are a lot of trouble," said Grandmother Sanders. "Anna will be helping, of course."

Lulu looked up at her grandmother. "Anna went to the city with her father for two days," she said. "They're visiting her uncle."

"That's nice," said Grandmother absent-mindedly. "I'm sure they'll have a lovely time."

Lulu thought about Anna and her father on a trip together. She remembered how much fun she had when she traveled with her father. Lulu's mother died when Lulu was three years old. Her father was a naturalist. Mr. Sanders traveled all over the world studying wild animals. After Lulu's mother died, Lulu went on trips with her dad. But when she turned ten, he said she had to live in one place. That's when Lulu moved in with her grandmother Sanders and met Anna and Pam. Lulu loved being a Pony Pal, but she missed being with her father and having her mother.

Lulu put her cereal bowl and juice glass in the dishwasher and went out to the paddock.

"Okay, ponies," she called. "Breakfast."

Snow White ran up to the paddock gate to meet her. Lulu brushed the mane off Snow White's eyes and kissed her forehead.

She fed the ponies and shoveled the pony plop. Next, she went into the shed to get Snow White's saddle.

"Lulu! Lulu!" she heard a girl call. "Look what I got!"

Six-year-old Rosalie Lacey and her brother, Mike, were coming toward the paddock.

Rosalie skipped happily beside her older brother. "I got a pet!" she shouted.

Lulu knew that Rosalie's mother thought animals were a lot of trouble and didn't like them. "No pets," was Mrs. Lacey's rule. Grandmother Sanders felt the same way about animals.

Mike and Rosalie met Lulu at the fence. Rosalie held up her hands, which were cupped into a ball. Tufts of golden fur stuck out between her fingers.

"What is it?" asked Lulu.

"It's a hamster," answered Mike.

"He's a Teddy Bear hamster," said Rosalie proudly. She opened her hands.

Lulu looked down on a little ball of golden fur with bright black eyes.

"His name is Alfie and he's mine," bragged Rosalie. "Isn't he cute?"

"He's adorable," agreed Lulu.

"The school had a bunch of extra ham-

4

sters," explained Mike. "Mom is letting Rosalie keep him on a trial basis. If Alfie's any trouble, back he goes." Mike put a hand on Rosalie's shoulder. "Right?"

"Alfie's *no* trouble," said Rosalie. She rubbed his fur against her cheek. "He's a good little boy."

"He wasn't good last night," Mike reminded Rosalie. He looked over at Lulu. "He got out of his cage. I found him in a box of pasta. He was eating it."

"What did your mother say?" asked Lulu.

"We're not telling her," said Rosalie. She smiled up at Mike. "It's our secret."

"If Mom knew Alfie got out, she'd never let Rosalie keep him," added Mike.

Snow White walked over to Lulu.

Rosalie held Alfie up so the pony could see him. "This is your new friend, Alfie," Rosalie told Snow White.

Lulu thought Snow White would startle and back away. But she didn't. Instead, she sniffed Alfie and nickered softly. Alfie's nose twitched curiously.

"They're already friends," bragged Rosalie. She looked around. "Where's Anna? I want to show Anna."

Lulu explained that Anna was gone for two days.

"I'll take care of Acorn while she's not here," offered Rosalie. "He can be *my* pony."

"Hey, great," said Mike. "If Rosalie's with you, I can — "

Lulu raised her right eyebrow. "You want me to baby-sit Rosalie so you can hang out with Tommy Rand," she said.

The Pony Pals didn't like Tommy Rand. And they didn't like Mike when he was with him. The two boys teased the Pony Pals and sometimes did stupid, dangerous things. Besides, thought Lulu, I'm going to Pam's.

"It's not baby-sitting if you're both playing with your ponies," protested Mike.

Lulu raised her eyebrow again. "Really?" she said. "I guess it's not baby-sitting if she's your sister, either."

"Forget it," said Mike.

"How come she's not playing with Mimi?" asked Lulu.

"Mimi's gone to her grandmother's for a few days," answered Mike.

Rosalie ignored them. She was busy making up a conversation between Alfie and Snow White.

"You shouldn't carry Alfie around in your hands like that," Lulu warned her. "He could escape again."

"He's mine," protested Rosalie. "He wants to be with me all the time."

A few minutes later, Mike, Rosalie, and Alfie left. Lulu rode Snow White onto Pony Pal Trail.

Pony Pal Trail was a mile-and-half trail through the woods. It led to Pam Crandal's place.

Lulu loved going to the Crandals'. Pam's father was a veterinarian and her mother was a riding teacher. There was always something interesting happening at the Crandals'. Lulu rode up to the barn. As she dismounted, Pam and her mother came out of the barn.

"Hi, Lulu," said Mrs. Crandal. "We're having a beginning rider clinic today and tomorrow. My assistant is sick, so Pam's helping."

"Sorry. I can't ride for a couple of days," Pam told Lulu.

Lulu didn't think Pam looked sorry. She looked happy. A car pulled into the driveway. Another followed. It was going to be a busy day at the Crandals'.

Lulu suddenly felt sad. Both her Pony Pals were doing something special with their parents. And hers was on another continent.

"Do you want to help with the clinic?" asked Pam.

"I can't," said Lulu. "I've got stuff to do."

Lulu remounted Snow White and rode back to Pony Pal Trail. If Dad was here, we'd do lots of stuff together, too, she thought.

Lulu's eyes filled with tears. It was hard to ride and cry at the same time. She halted Snow White under a tree and slid off. Lulu reached into her pocket and pulled out a folded envelope. It was a letter from her father. He was studying elephants in Africa. When he finished that, he was going to India to study tigers. Lulu wouldn't see him for two more months. She tried to read the letter again, but she couldn't. The words were all blurry through her tears.

Snow White nudged Lulu's shoulder and nickered sympathetically. Lulu leaned her head against her pony's neck. "My father is far, far away," she whispered in a choked voice. "And all my friends are busy."

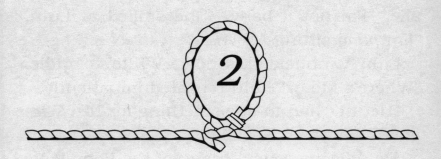

What Time Is It?

As Lulu led Snow White through the paddock gate, she heard Rosalie Lacey's voice.

"Bow for me, Acorn," Rosalie said. "You do it for Anna."

Mike and Rosalie are back, thought Lulu. But she only saw Rosalie in front of the shed with Acorn.

"Where's Mike?" Lulu asked the younger girl.

"Gone," answered Rosalie.

"I told him I couldn't baby-sit you," said Lulu.

"You don't have to baby-sit me," said Rosalie. "I'm not a baby." She smiled at Lulu. "I'm *pony*-sitting Acorn."

Lulu unbuckled Snow White's bridle. "Where's Mike?" Lulu repeated impatiently.

"He, uh, had to do something for Ms. Wiggins," answered Rosalie.

Ms. Wiggins was a friend of the Pony Pals. She had a lot of land and wonderful riding trails. The Pony Pals could ride there whenever they wanted. That's what I'll do this afternoon, thought Lulu. I'll ride on Ms. Wiggins's trails.

"When's Mike coming back for you?" asked Lulu.

"He's coming back in . . . an hour," said Rosalie. She patted Acorn's neck. "I told him I'd wait here."

Lulu took off Snow White's saddle and brought it to the tack room in the shed. Rosalie followed with the bridle and reins. Acorn followed Rosalie.

"Can Acorn and me ride with you later?" asked Roslie. "Acorn wants to."

"I can't ride alone with you," explained Lulu. "It's too big a responsibility."

Rosalie leaned her head against Acorn's neck. "Okay," she said softly. "Alfie and me won't go riding." She reached into her sweatshirt pocket and gave out a little yelp.

"Did Alfie bite you?" asked Lulu.

Rosalie looked around desperately. "He's gone!" she cried.

"I told you — " Lulu began to say. But she stopped herself. It wasn't the time to scold Rosalie. They had to focus on finding Alfie.

"You look in the paddock," directed Lulu. "I'll look in the shed."

Lulu checked the floor. No Alfie.

She looked in all the corners. The missing hamster wasn't there, either.

Meanwhile, Rosalie searched the paddock. Acorn followed her around. "Alfie! Alfie!" Rosalie called between sobs. "Where are you?"

Lulu ran over to the younger girl and put a hand on her shoulder. "Rosalie, this isn't the time to cry," she said in a very calm voice. "You won't be able to see Alfie if you're crying."

"But what if I *don't* find him?" cried Rosalie.

"Think about *finding* him," said Lulu. "It's the only idea you should have in your head."

Rosalie wiped her tears with her sleeve. "Okay," she agreed.

Lulu turned back to the shed. Where should I look next? she wondered.

She took Rosalie's hand. "Come on," she whispered. "I need your help. We're going to look in the tack room."

Rosalie's eyes widened. "Maybe he's in there," she said softly.

Lulu and Rosalie quietly opened the door to the small tack room in the back of the walk-in shed. Snow White followed them.

"I'll open the feed box," Lulu whispered to Rosalie. "If he's in there, you grab him."

"Okay," agreed Rosalie.

Lulu opened the lid. But she didn't see the hamster.

Snow White nickered as if to say, "He's in there. Keep looking."

Lulu leaned into the feed box and looked

more closely. A small lump in the bag of grain moved. Lulu pointed to it.

"Alfie!" Rosalie whispered excitedly.

"Ready?" asked Lulu.

Rosalie nodded.

Lulu quickly opened the bag. The hamster was crawling around on top of the feed. His cheeks were puffy with grain. Rosalie grabbed him and cuddled him against her chest.

Lulu patted Snow White's head. "Good work, Snow White," she said. She turned to Rosalie. "Hold on to Alfie and don't put him in your pocket again. I think we better make him a travel box."

Lulu and Rosalie went into the house and up to Lulu's bedroom. Lulu looked around her room for a small box for Alfie. Her grandmother had given her a big box of stationery. Lulu emptied out the paper and envelopes. She held the box up to show Rosalie. "This will be perfect," she said.

They sat on Lulu's bed and Rosalie held Alfie. Lulu was putting holes in the top of the box when her grandmother walked in.

"Hi, Rosalie," Ms. Sanders said cheerfully.

Before Lulu could stop her, Rosalie held up her hamster. "This is Alfie," she announced proudly. "He's my pet."

Grandmother Sanders gave out a little scream and jumped back. "A rat!" she cried.

"He's not a rat," protested Rosalie. "He's a hamster."

Grandmother glared at Lulu. "I told you no animals in the house!" she said angrily.

Lulu took Alfie from Rosalie and quickly put him in the box.

"Hamsters are *rodents*," said Grandmother with a shudder. "Get it out of here!"

"Sorry, Grandma," said Lulu as she stood up. "We'll go outside."

Rosalie followed Lulu out of the room.

"My grandmother is really afraid of mice and stuff," Lulu explained as they walked down the stairs.

"She shouldn't be afraid of Alfie," protested Rosalie. "He's cute."

"But she is," said Lulu.

The girls sat side by side on the porch

swing. Alfie's new box lay between them. The clock tower rang out twelve gongs.

"It's twelve o'clock," said Lulu. "Where's Mike?"

"He'll be here pretty soon," said Rosalie.

"If it's twelve P.M. here," Lulu told Rosalie. "It's five P.M. where my father is. He's in Africa."

"My father's in Chicago," said Rosalie with a sigh. "What time is it there?"

Lulu thought for a moment. "It's eleven A.M. in Chicago," she answered.

"My dad is never, ever going to live with us again," Rosalie said sadly. "I want to go to Chicago. But it's too much money."

Lulu pushed the porch swing with her foot. She felt sorry for Rosalie. She knew what it was like to miss your dad.

"We have two things in common, Rosalie," she said. "One, both our dads are far away. And two, your mother and my grandmother don't like animals."

Rosalie held up three fingers. "We have *three* things alike," she said.

"What's the third?' asked Lulu.

Rosalie grinned. "We both like ponies."

Lulu smiled back at her. "That's true," she agreed.

Lulu unclipped the barrette from her own hair. She turned the shiny pink barrette over in her hand. It was shaped like a butterfly.

"That's pretty," said Rosalie.

"You can have it," said Lulu.

Rosalie beamed. "I can?" she exclaimed happily.

Lulu clipped the barrette onto Rosalie's hair.

Ten minutes later, Rosalie and Lulu were still on the porch. Alfie was still sleeping. And Mike still wasn't there.

"You can go, Lulu," Rosalie told her. "I can wait here for Mike by myself. I always wait for Mike."

Lulu knew that was true. The Pony Pals often saw Rosalie waiting for her brother.

"Well . . . okay," agreed Lulu. "Thanks."

Lulu rode for an hour on Ms. Wiggins's trails. It was lonely riding without her Pony

Pals. I'll ride over to Ms. Wiggins's and say hi, she decided.

Lulu saw Ms. Wiggins before she reached the house. Ms. Wiggins had an easel set up in the field and was painting a landscape. She waved when she saw Lulu.

Lulu rode up to her.

"Hello, there," said Ms. Wiggins. "I thought you were watching Rosalie this afternoon."

"Who said that?" asked Lulu.

"Mike," answered Ms. Wiggins. "He came by to borrow a fishing pole. He went fishing with Tommy Rand."

"Rosalie is waiting for Mike on my grandmother's porch," said Lulu. "He was supposed to pick her up more than an hour ago."

"I'm surprised at Mike," said Ms. Wiggins. "He's usually a very responsible boy."

Except when Tommy Rand is around, thought Lulu.

Pony Detective

"I'm going to ride over to the lake and tell Mike to go get Rosalie," said Lulu.

"Do you want to call your grandmother first?" asked Ms. Wiggins. "Maybe Rosalie can wait in the beauty parlor."

"Good idea," agreed Lulu.

Snow White stayed with Ms. Wiggins while Lulu ran into the house to call the beauty parlor.

Grandmother Sanders told Lulu that Rosalie was not on the porch.

"Can you check the paddock, please?" asked Lulu.

Grandmother Sanders didn't see Rosalie in the paddock, either. "And Acorn's not there," added Grandmother.

"Uh-oh," said Lulu. "I bet Rosalie took Acorn out for a ride. I have to find her."

Lulu hung up and went back out to tell Ms. Wiggins.

"I'll drive to the lake and tell Mike," said Ms. Wiggins. "We'll look for Rosalie and Acorn in town."

"I'll call Pam," added Lulu. "We'll search on the trails."

"Let's meet back at your place," said Ms. Wiggins as she closed her paint box. "Whoever finds Rosalie should bring her straight there."

If we find her, thought Lulu.

Half an hour later, Lulu and Snow White met Pam and Lightning on Pony Pal Trail at the three birch trees.

"I should have stayed with Rosalie until

Mike came," Lulu told Pam. "And I was supposed to be taking care of Acorn. Now, they're *both* missing."

"Rosalie's a good rider," Pam reminded Lulu. "And Acorn is really smart."

"But Rosalie's never ridden alone," said Lulu. "What if she's doing something stupid, like running away? She's had an hour-and-a-half head start. What if she gets hurt?"

"Where do you think we should look for her?" asked Pam.

"On Pony Pal Trail going toward my place," suggested Lulu. "You look for clues on the right side of the trail. I'll look on the left." Lulu leaned forward and patted her pony's neck. "We need you to help us find Rosalie and Acorn, Snow White."

The two girls rode slowly and checked the ground and bushes for clues.

Pam was the first to find one. It was a pile of pony plop in the middle of the trail. The girls dismounted and went over to it.

"Maybe Snow White did it," said Pam. "You came this way three times today."

Lulu studied the plop. "It's very fresh," she said. "I bet Acorn did it."

The two friends checked the area carefully. Lulu spotted something bright pink in the bushes. A shiny pink butterfly barrette was stuck on a branch.

"I found another clue," Lulu called to Pam. She showed Pam the barrette. "I gave this barrette to Rosalie today."

A smaller trail started beside the bush. Snow White pulled toward it.

"Let's follow Snow White," suggested Lulu. She tied Snow White's reins around the saddle horn and patted her rump. "Go ahead, Snow White."

Snow White walked and sniffed her way along the narrow trail. When the trail branched in two, Snow White went to the right. Lulu, Pam, and Lightning followed her.

In a few minutes, the trail ended at the edge of Badd Brook. Lulu saw Anna's handsome brown-and-black pony, Acorn, drinking from the brook.

Rosalie lay on a rock, fast asleep. Alfie's travel box was on her belly.

"I'll wake her up," said Lulu.

Snow White joined Acorn. Pam led Lightning to the brook while Lulu went over to Rosalie. She put a hand on the girl's shoulder. "Wake up, Rosalie," she said softly.

Rosalie opened her eyes and stared up at Lulu. "Acorn wanted to go for a ride," she blurted out.

"*Rosalie* wanted to go for a ride," said Lulu crossly.

Rosalie sat up and saw Pam, Lightning, and Snow White.

"Everybody's here," she said happily.

"Did you tell Mike I would watch you this afternoon?" asked Lulu.

Rosalie nodded. "He had to put out the garbage," she explained. "When he came back I said you called on the telephone. I said you wanted me to come right over."

"Then you told *me* he was picking you up in an hour," said Lulu. "But that wasn't true, either."

"I know," said Rosalie.

"And you took Acorn out, all by yourself," added Lulu.

Rosalie nodded.

Pam came over. Rosalie took Alfie out of his box and held him up. "This is my hamster," she bragged. "His name is Alfie."

Pam ignored Alfie. "You lied to Lulu and to Mike. Then you took someone else's pony and didn't tell anyone. You could have gotten hurt."

"Acorn and I wanted to go for a ride," said Rosalie.

Lulu could feel herself getting angrier and angrier with Rosalie. I'm glad she isn't my sister, she thought. For a second, Lulu even felt sorry for Mike.

"We'd better ride back," Lulu told Pam.

"Oh, goodie," said Rosalie, jumping up. "I'm going to ride with the Pony Pals."

The three girls led the ponies to Pony Pal Trail. Lulu and Snow White went first. Rosalie, Alfie, and Acorn followed. Pam and Lightning were last.

Lulu and Pam didn't talk to Rosalie on the slow ride home. But Rosalie didn't seem to care. She hummed happily to herself and talked to Alfie and Acorn.

When they reached the paddock, Rosalie took off Acorn's tack all by herself and gave him a good rubdown. After Lulu took off Snow White's tack, she ran to the beauty parlor.

A woman was under the hair dryer. Grandmother Sanders was sweeping up black hair.

"Rosalie and Acorn are safe," Lulu announced.

"Thank goodness," said Grandmother. She shook a finger at Lulu. "You see the kind of trouble children get into with animals. I hope you're planning to tell Rosalie's mother what she did."

Rosalie will get in serious trouble if I tell her mother, thought Lulu. Her mom will probably even make her take Alfie back to the school.

Can I do that to Rosalie? she wondered. Will Mike?

A Pony Ride

Lulu hurried back to the paddock. Ms. Wiggins, Mike, and Tommy were already there.

"Rosalie, you know you aren't allowed to take Acorn out by yourself," scolded Mike.

"What's the big deal?" asked Tommy. "She knows how to ride. I think it's pretty funny." He laughed and patted Rosalie on the back.

Lulu glared at Tommy. "It's not funny," she said.

"Your mother is going to have a fit, Rosie," said Tommy with another laugh.

"If you tell, she won't let me keep Alfie!" wailed Rosalie.

Pam and Lulu exchanged a glance. They knew that Rosalie was right. Mrs. Lacey wouldn't let her keep Alfie. And she'd be furious at Mike.

"I don't want my mother to know," Mike whispered to Lulu.

"Okay," agreed Lulu.

Mike put an arm around Rosalie's shoulders. "Don't cry, okay?" She looked up at him. "We won't tell her," he said. "Come on. We're going home."

"Hey, man. What about fishing?" asked Tommy. "And our bikes are at the lake."

"I have to take care of Rosalie now," said Mike. "I'll get my bike tomorrow."

"Rosalie can stay with the Pony Pests," said Tommy. He smiled his phony grin at Pam and Lulu. "Baby-sitting is girls' work. Tell him you'll do it."

"No," shouted Lulu and Pam in unison. "We won't."

Tommy glared at Rosalie. "Rosalie, you're a pain," he said.

"Let's go, Tommy," Ms. Wiggins said sternly. "I'll give you a ride to the lake." Even Ms. Wiggins was annoyed with Tommy Rand. She put a hand on Mike's shoulder, said good-bye, and left with Tommy.

Mike looked at the Pony Pals. "Thanks for finding my sister," he said.

Lulu woke up later than usual the next morning. I'll feed the ponies before I eat breakfast, she thought as she got out of bed. As Lulu dressed, she remembered that in a few hours Anna would be back, and Pam would be finished with the riding clinic. It would be great to be with her Pony Pals again.

Lulu was halfway to the paddock when she saw Rosalie. "C'mon, Acorn," Rosalie said. "Bow for me. I know you can do it." Rosalie was trying to get Acorn to do tricks. Again. Just like the day before.

"Mike left you here *again*," said Lulu angrily. "I told him —" It felt like yesterday was replaying like a movie. She noticed Alfie's travel box opened and empty on the ground. "And where's Alfie?"

"Mike's in bed and Alfie is going for a ride," said Rosalie. She pointed to Snow White's neck. "He's having a pony ride."

Alfie was sitting on Snow White's mane. It was cute, but Lulu wasn't amused. "Put him back in his box," she said sternly.

"But — " Rosalie started to say.

"Now!" insisted Lulu.

Rosalie took Alfie out of Snow White's mane and put him back in his box.

Snow White lowered her head and sniffed the closed box. She nickered as if to say, "Hi in there."

"Why did Mike let you come over here?" asked Lulu.

"I told you. He's sleeping," said Rosalie impatiently. Rosalie reached into her pocket and pulled out a folded piece of paper.

"Look," she said. "I wrote Mike a note so he won't be mad."

Lulu opened the paper.

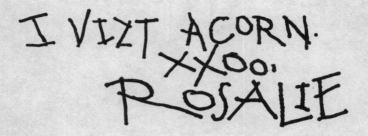

I VIZT ACORN.
XXOO.
ROSALIE

Lulu gave the piece of paper back to Rosalie. "Why do you still have the note if it's for Mike?" she asked.

"Oops," said Rosalie. "I forgot to leave it."

Lulu picked up Alfie's box with one hand and took Rosalie's hand with the other. "Come on," she said. "I'm taking you home."

Halfway across the Town Green they saw Mike coming toward them. He looked furious. Rosalie ran to him, waving the note. Lulu turned around and went back to the paddock. She wondered if Mike would tell on Rosalie this time.

When Lulu finally fed the ponies, Snow White gobbled down her grain. Acorn ate more slowly. That's strange, thought Lulu. Acorn usually eats faster than Snow White. Lulu patted Acorn's side. "You must miss Anna," she said.

After her breakfast, Lulu went back outside and cleaned up the paddock. She also cleaned out the little tack room and polished the saddles. She wanted everything perfect when Anna came home.

That afternoon, Lulu sat on the tree swing in the Harleys' yard. She read a book of horse stories while she waited for Anna. Lulu and Pam loved to read about ponies and horses. Anna didn't like to read as much as they did. She was dyslexic, so reading and writing were difficult for her. Anna loved to draw and paint and listen to books on tape about ponies and horses.

Lulu was halfway through her book when Anna finally came home. Lulu met her at the car. She told Anna everything that happened while she was gone.

"Rosalie wishes Acorn was her pony," said Anna thoughtfully.

"She sure does," agreed Lulu. "Her hamster is real cute, but you can't ride a hamster."

The two friends went out to their ponies.

"Hey, Acorn, I'm back," called Anna.

Acorn didn't look up.

"You, silly," said Anna as she went through the gate. "Are you playing a game?"

Anna went over to her pony. He looked up at her, but he didn't nicker or act excited.

Anna studied him closely. "What's wrong with Acorn?" she asked.

Exterminator

Lulu looked at Acorn carefully, too. "He ate really slowly this morning," she told Anna. "I thought he missed you."

"I'll get him something to eat now," said Anna.

While Anna was in the shed, Pam rode out of Pony Pal Trail. "Is Anna back?" she asked as she dismounted.

At that instant, Anna came out of the shed. She held up an empty box of treats. "This box was full when I left," she said.

"I didn't feed Acorn any treats," answered

Lulu. "Just an apple last night. It must have been Rosalie. She was trying to get him to do tricks for her."

"Acorn isn't acting right," Anna explained to Pam.

Anna rubbed Acorn's neck. He nudged her shoulder.

"Do you have a tummy ache?" asked Anna. "I'm here now. I'll take care of you."

"I'm sorry that he ate too much," said Lulu.

"It's not your fault," said Anna. "It's Rosalie's fault."

"Speak of the devil," said Pam, pointing to the driveway.

Mike and Rosalie met the Pony Pals at the fence. Rosalie looked at the ground instead of at the Pony Pals. Mike poked her. "Say it," he muttered.

"I'm sorry," said Rosalie softly. She looked up at Lulu. "I did bad things. I'm really and truly and very really sorry."

Lulu's heart softened. "I accept your apology," she said.

"And I — uh, have to ask a favor," said Mike. "My bike's still at the lake. I've got to go pick it up." Mike looked pleadingly at the Pony Pals. "I'll come right back. I promise."

The Pony Pals exchanged a glance. It was their chance to talk to Rosalie about over-feeding Acorn. Pam nodded.

"Okay, Mike. You go get your bike," said Lulu. "Rosalie can stay with us."

"Thanks," he said.

"Can I ride Acorn?" asked Rosalie.

"No!" the Pony Pals answered in unison.

"We'll be at my house," Lulu told Mike.

Rosalie held up Alfie's travel box and grinned at Anna. "I have a pet!" she announced. "His name is Alfie."

Anna looked inside the box. "He's very cute," she said. "But he'd be happier sleeping at home."

"He wants to be with me," said Rosalie stubbornly. "He doesn't like to stay home."

Rosalie closed the top to Alfie's box and followed Anna and Lulu to the house.

The four girls sat around the kitchen table.

"We have something important to talk to you about," began Lulu.

"You gave Acorn too many treats," Pam told Rosalie. "Now he has a tummy ache."

Pam told Rosalie that a girl once fed Lightning too many apples. "Lightning was very sick and could have died," she concluded.

"Is Acorn *very* sick?" asked Rosalie.

"No," admitted Anna. "But I can't take him out riding today. And if you had kept overfeeding him, he would be."

"Taking care of pets is a big responsibility," added Lulu.

"I know," said Rosalie. She reached to the floor for Alfie's box. "I take *very* good care of Alfie." She opened up the box to show off Alfie again.

The box was empty and there was a hole eaten out of one corner.

"He's gone!" screamed Rosalie.

"Uh-oh," Lulu said. "Let's search,"

Lulu and Anna crawled around on their hands and knees looking in all the corners. Pam opened the cupboards. Rosalie was trying to see under the refrigerator.

"What's going on?" asked a woman's voice. Lulu looked up and saw her grandmother standing over her. "Did someone lose something?"

"I lost Alfie," Rosalie answered before Lulu could stop her.

Grandmother yelped and ran out of the kitchen and onto the back porch. She looked in at the girls through the screen door. "Lulu, I told you that rodent could not come into this house," she shouted.

Lulu went over to the screen door. "We'll find him, Grandma," she said.

Grandmother nervously peeked in through the screen door before coming back inside.

"All I wanted was a cup of tea before my next client," she said. "But there's a *rat* in my kitchen."

"Alfie's not a — " Rosalie began to say.

41

Lulu put a hand over Rosalie's mouth.

"I'll make you a cup of tea, Mrs. Sanders," offered Pam.

"We'll bring it to the beauty parlor," added Lulu.

"And we'll find Alfie," said Lulu. "I promise, Grandma."

Grandmother Sanders glared at Lulu. "I will not have rodents in my house." She looked around at all four girls. "I'm calling an exterminator."

Grandmother left the kitchen, and Rosalie Lacey burst into tears.

Three Ideas

Pam put the water on for tea. Lulu placed a tea bag in her grandmother's favorite teapot.

"Keep looking for Alfie," Lulu instructed Anna and Rosalie.

Lulu put a pink napkin, the teapot, a cup, a plate of cookies, and a small bunch of grapes on a silver tray.

Rosalie tugged on Lulu's arm. "Don't let your grandma call that ex-ermin-ator person," she pleaded.

"I'll try," said Lulu. She carefully carried the tea tray to the front of the house.

Grandmother was sitting at her desk looking through the phone book. She looked up and saw the beautiful tea tray.

"Don't try to butter me up, Lucinda," she said. "You know I don't like animals. And I'm terrified of rodents."

"I know, Grandma," said Lulu as she put the tray on the desk. "But Rosalie loves animals and she's never had a pet before. She'd be so upset if you killed Alfie."

"I wouldn't do it myself," said Grandmother. She pointed to an ad in the yellow pages of the phone book. "It's a job for Rid-All exterminators."

"Please give us time to look for Alfie," said Lulu.

"My mind is made up, Lucinda," said Grandmother. "I'm calling them right now." Grandmother picked up the phone and held it to her ear. She tapped the phone button several times. "That's strange," she said. "There's no dial tone. The phone line is dead."

"Maybe it's a sign you shouldn't call the exterminator," said Lulu. She smiled at her grandmother. "Please give us more time to look for Alfie, Grandma. Rosalie's parents are divorced and her dad lives in Chicago. She practically never sees him and she misses him. Alfie makes her happy."

"Well, I can't even phone an exterminator right now, can I?" said Grandmother. "I can't even call the telephone company to say that the phone doesn't work. And I have another client in five minutes."

Grandmother sipped her tea and thought. "I'll give you until tomorrow morning to find that creature," she said. "But I'm making an appointment with the exterminator — in case you don't find him. Meanwhile, I'd better figure out what's wrong with this phone."

Lulu went back to the kitchen. Mike had joined the search. They hadn't found Alfie. Rosalie's face was tearstained.

Lulu put an arm around her shoulder. "Don't worry, Rosalie," she said. "We'll find him."

Rosalie and Mike had to go to meet their mother after work.

"Will she notice that Alfie is missing?" Pam asked Mike and Rosalie.

"She never looks in his cage," answered Mike.

"She thinks he's creepy," added Rosalie. She looked over at Lulu. "She's scared, too, like your grandma."

As soon as Rosalie and Mike were gone, the Pony Pals had an emergency meeting.

"We should have a sleepover here tonight," said Lulu.

"And let's fix dinner for your grandmother," suggested Anna.

"Good idea," agreed Pam. "We can eat in the dining room. That way she won't have to come in the kitchen at all."

"And we need three ideas for finding Alfie," added Lulu.

"We can share those after dinner," said Anna.

"If we haven't found him by then," added Lulu.

Anna stood up. "I have to go check on Acorn," she said, "and tell my parents I'm sleeping here. I'll call your mother, too, Pam."

While Anna was gone, Lulu looked behind the plates and in all the cups for Alfie. He wasn't there.

Pam put her ear to the floor and listened. "I don't hear anything," she said. Lulu took a water glass off the counter and knelt beside Pam. She put the open side of the glass to the floor and put her ear to the other side. She didn't hear anything, either. I wish I could hear as well as Snow White, she thought.

Anna came back. "Acorn is okay," she announced. "He ate all his grain. I fed Snow White, too."

"Thanks," said Lulu.

Anna sat down and drew. Lulu knew she was working on her idea.

Pam looked behind and under the spice rack. Alfie wasn't there.

Meanwhile, Lulu looked in every corner of the pots-and-pans drawer. Alfie wasn't there, either.

"We've looked everywhere," said Lulu. She felt discouraged.

48

"The broom closet!" said Pam. "We haven't looked there." She carefully opened the broom closet door. "I'll search it."

"Anna and I will start dinner," Lulu told Pam.

Lulu took a jar of spaghetti sauce and a box of pasta out of the cupboard. She checked the box for chew marks and opened the box carefully. Alfie wasn't there.

Pam didn't find Alfie in the broom closet. But when she finished looking, she wrote something in her pocket notebook.

I'm the only one who doesn't have an idea, thought Lulu. A few minutes later, an idea finally came to her. She wrote it down on the telephone pad.

During dinner, Grandmother kept her feet on a chair. She didn't mention Alfie once. But she said three times that she wasn't going into the kitchen. And she announced that the telephone company would be coming in the morning. "And the exterminator will be here at ten-thirty A.M.," she added.

After dinner, the girls sat around the kitchen table. It was time to share their ideas for finding Alfie.

"I'll start," said Pam. She handed her idea to Lulu who read it out loud.

Maybe Alfie ate through the telephone wire. We should look where the wires go.

"Do hamsters eat telephone wires?" asked Anna.

"Rodents can," answered Pam. "And a hamster is a rodent. They have very sharp teeth. Mice ate through the telephone line in our barn once."

"How will your idea help us find Alfie?" asked Anna.

"He might be in the walls or under the floorboards," said Pam. "If we follow the wires, maybe we can see where he went."

"How are we going to get him out if he's under the floor or in the walls?" asked Lulu.

"That's the hard part," answered Pam. She turned to Anna. "What's your idea?"

Anna opened her pocket sketchbook and put it on the table between Pam and Lulu.

"Hamsters sleep all day and play all night. Right?" asked Anna.

"Right," agreed Lulu and Pam.

"We haven't found Alfie yet because he's sleeping," explained Anna. "At night, he'll run around and do things. We'll hear him. Nighttime is the best time to look for him."

"Good idea," said Pam. "We'll stay up all night if we have to."

"What's your idea, Lulu?" asked Anna.

Remove anything a hamster would eat from the cabinets. Then put food and water out for Alfie.

"That's a great idea," said Pam. "What do you think his favorite food is?"

"He loves the ponies' grain," said Lulu.

Anna looked around the kitchen and sighed. "The awful thing is, Alfie might not even be in the house," she said. "He could have gone out under the screen door."

"He might be far away from here by now," added Pam.

"And we might never find him," added Lulu.

The "Don't Go To Sleep" Sleepover

Grandmother Sanders said good night to the girls and went to her bedroom to watch television. It was time for the Pony Pals to try their ideas.

First, they took all the dry food out of the kitchen cabinets and put it on the dining room table.

Next, Lulu went to the shed for horse feed. When Acorn saw her, he ran around the edge of the paddock. He's his old self again, thought Lulu.

Snow White walked over to Lulu. Lulu patted her pony's neck. "We can't find your pal, Alfie," she said. She wished that Snow White could help them in their search.

Lulu scooped some grain into a cup and went back inside. Pam and Anna were crawling around on the kitchen floor.

"Did you find anything?" Lulu asked as she poured feed into the saucer.

"No," said Anna as she stood up.

"We followed the phone line all the way from your grandmother's shop," said Pam. "It wasn't chewed on or anything."

Lulu put the saucer of feed and a saucer of water in the empty cabinet. She left the door to the cabinet half open.

"Maybe the phone is out for a different reason," said Pam. "Maybe it's just a coincidence."

"Good point," agreed Anna.

Anna looked out the window. "It's nighttime," she said. "If Alfie's in the house some-place, maybe he'll wake up now."

"We should watch and listen in every room," suggested Pam. "Lulu, you're the best detective. You stay in the kitchen."

"Okay," agreed Lulu.

"I'll stake out the living room and dining room," said Pam.

"And I'll go to the hair salon," added Anna.

Lulu put feed into two baggies and gave them to Pam and Anna. "Put food out for him," she instructed.

"If he comes out, do we just try to grab him?" asked Anna.

"We need equipment for that," said Lulu. She opened a drawer and took out three small plastic containers with tops. She handed one each to Anna and Pam and kept one for her-self. "Use these to catch him," she instructed. "Then we'll put him in his travel box."

"He ate through that box," said Lulu. Pam held up a big round cookie tin from the drawer. "How about this?"

"Perfect," said Anna. "All we need is a top with air holes."

Lulu found a strainer that fit over the top of the container.

Next, they put in torn paper towels and some feed. They left the new travel container on the table. It was time for the nighttime patrol.

Lulu stood at attention. "Troops, prepare," she announced in a pretend-adult voice.

Pam and Anna picked up their small containers in one hand and baggie of feed in the other.

"Attention!" ordered Lulu.

Pam and Anna stood at attention.

"Ready!"

They turned on their heels.

"March!"

They strode out of the room to their posts.

Lulu sat on the kitchen floor facing the open cabinet and listened carefully. After a half hour she heard a scraping noise inside the cabinet. She saw the top of a furry little head. Alfie! she thought. I hope I can catch him.

But it wasn't the fluffy golden hamster that was eating the food. It was a small gray mouse.

Lulu pounced and caught the mouse in the plastic container. She held the top over the opening.

"Sorry, mouse," she said as she kicked the screen door open. "But my grandmother doesn't want animals in her house. Especially rodents."

Lulu dropped the mouse outside in the bushes.

When Anna and Pam came back to the kitchen, Lulu told them about the mouse.

Anna made a face. "That would have given me the creeps," she said.

Pam crawled her fingertips up Anna's arm. "That mouse would have crawled all over you," she said in a spooky voice.

"Ew — w!" said Anna as she pulled her arm away. With her other hand she tickled Pam around her waist. "He'd get you, too."

Pam, who was very ticklish, giggled.

Lulu joined in the tickle attack.

Grandmother's booming voice interrupted them. "Did you find that creature yet?" she called from upstairs.

Lulu went to the foot of the back stairs and looked up. "Not yet, Grandma," she said. "But we will. Don't worry."

All tickling stopped.

"Were there *any* clues in your rooms?" Lulu asked Anna and Pam.

"I thought I heard Alfie in the living room," said Pam. "But it was just the grandfather clock ticking."

"All I could hear were cars going by and the TV in your grandmother's room," said Anna.

"And all I heard was that mouse and the refrigerator," added Lulu.

Grandmother said good night to the girls. "Don't stay up too late," she added.

They called back, "Good night. We won't."

The girls listened for Grandmother Sanders to go back to her room.

59

Lulu sat on the floor facing the open cabinet. Anna and Pam sat at the table.

"What do we do next?" asked Pam. "How do we find Alfie?"

Anna opened the freezer door. "Hm-m," she said thoughtfully. "How about some chocolate ice cream? I always think better when I've had some ice cream."

"Me, too," agreed Pam.

Pam and Anna sat on the floor with Lulu to eat their ice cream.

"I'm glad we're not taking turns staying up," said Anna.

"It's more fun when we all stay awake," agreed Lulu.

"So what can we do next to find Alfie?" asked Pam. "None of our ideas worked."

"I bet Snow White could find him," said Lulu. "Ponies have better hearing and smell than people."

"But Snow White is outside," said Pam.

"I know," said Lulu with a grin.

"You'd bring Snow White into the house?" exclaimed Anna.

"Snow White likes Alfie," continued Lulu thoughtfully. "She found him when he ran away before."

"I've never heard of a pony or a horse *liking* a hamster," said Pam.

"Snow White really does like Alfie," insisted Lulu.

"What if your grandmother found out Snow White was in the house?" said Anna. "She'd be so upset and angry. She was furious when Acorn got in her garden. That wasn't even inside the house."

"We have to be sure she doesn't find out," said Lulu.

The Pony Pals worked out a plan. If they hadn't found Alfie by midnight, Pam and Lulu would go to the paddock and get Snow White. Anna would stay in the hall upstairs near grandmother's bedroom.

"Remember you'll be acting a part, Anna," said Lulu. "Put on your pajamas and wait in the hall. If my grandmother wakes up, pretend you had a nightmare. Talk real loud so she won't hear Snow White."

"And we'll know that she's awake," added Pam. "But how do we know when she's asleep?"

"She snores," said Lulu. "I'll go listen."

At midnight, Lulu went upstairs and put her ear to her grandmother's door. Even through the closed door she could hear snoring.

Lulu sneaked quietly back downstairs. "She's asleep," she announced.

Anna went to her post upstairs and Lulu and Pam went out to the paddock.

"Snow White can be shy," Pam reminded Lulu. "I hope she isn't afraid of going in the house."

"Do you have the carrot?" asked Lulu.

Pam patted her pocket. "I do," she answered. Then she went into the shed to get two empty pails.

Meanwhile, Lulu clipped a lead rope to Snow White's halter. "Let's go, Snow White," she said. "We're going to search for Alfie."

Lulu led Snow White out of the paddock, through the Harleys' yard, and up the driveway. There was a ramp at the front of the house leading to the front door. Pam followed behind with two pails.

"What if someone sees us?" asked Lulu.

Just then, a car drove by. The driver slowed down when she saw the white pony on the porch.

Lulu waved her on. She didn't recognize the driver.

"It's an out-of-state license plate," said Pam.

"That was a close call," giggled Lulu. She suddenly felt very silly bringing a pony into the house.

Pam was giggling, too, as she opened the front door.

Snow White wasn't amused and didn't want to go into the house.

"Come on, Snow White," said Lulu. "Everything is going to be okay."

Pam held out a carrot. Snow White sniffed and followed the carrot through the front door.

In the Kitchen

Lulu was glad the hall was carpeted. Snow White's hooves would not make much noise on the soft surface. But what if Snow White does her business on the carpet? thought Lulu. She signaled Pam to go behind Snow White with the pails.

Snow White followed Lulu and the carrot into the kitchen.

First, Snow White ate the carrot reward.

Next, she made a mess in the pail.

Lulu squinched up her nose. "I hope my grandmother doesn't smell that," she said.

Pam put the used pail on the back porch.

Snow White looked around the kitchen curiously. Lulu held out Alfie's empty travel box. Snow White sniffed it and nickered as if to say, "Where is he?"

"Sh-sh," Lulu told her pony. She stroked her mane.

Snow White's tail swished. Grandmother's favorite mug slid across the counter. Lulu lunged for the mug and caught it halfway to the floor.

She heard Anna's voice on the second floor. Anna sounded terrified. "There was a monster," she cried.

Lulu froze and listened. Snow White's ears went forward. Lulu rubbed her pony's side. Please don't make any noise, Snow White, she prayed. It's only Anna acting.

"The monster had awful yellow eyes," continued Anna. " And it was chasing me. It was going to kill me."

Lulu couldn't look at Pam. If she did she knew she would start laughing. She moved closer to the stairs. She wanted to hear what Grandmother said to Anna.

"You've had a nightmare, Anna," Grandmother said. "Why don't you go back to bed? I'm going downstairs for some warm milk. I'll bring you some, too."

Pam and Lulu exchanged a terrified glance.

"You shouldn't go to the kitchen," said Anna quickly. "We didn't find the hamster yet. I'll get your milk."

A moment later, Anna was in the kitchen. Her mouth fell open when she saw Snow White. "She's so big in here," she whispered. "Did she find Alfie?"

"No," Pam answered.

"Your grandmother wants warm milk," Anna told Lulu. She looked curiously at the empty counter. "She said her mug is on the counter."

Lulu held out the mug she'd caught. "Here it is," she said.

Lulu warmed some milk in the microwave and handed the mug to Anna.

Anna went back upstairs with it.

"This was a stupid idea," Lulu whispered to Pam. "Snow White's not going to find Alfie. Let's get her out of here."

"Okay," agreed Pam.

Lulu reached for Snow White's halter to turn her around. But Snow White didn't budge. Instead, she lowered her head toward the open cabinet.

Lulu gave a little tug of the halter and Snow White finally raised her head.

Pam pointed to Snow White's head and giggled. "Look!" she whispered.

Lulu turned and came eye to eye with Alfie. He was sitting in Snow White's mane, his cheeks bulging with feed.

"Alfie!" exclaimed Lulu.

Snow White nickered proudly.

"Sh-sh!" said Pam.

"Quick," whispered Lulu. "Let's get her out of here."

Pam carefully lifted Alfie off Snow White and put him in the cookie tin.

Lulu turned her pony around and led her down the hall. She heard the front stairs creak. Grandma! thought Lulu. She'll be so angry. What if she makes me give up Snow White?

Her heart pounding, Lulu looked up the stairs. Anna was coming down them.

"We found Alfie," whispered Pam. She handed the cookie tin to Anna.

"All right!" Anna started to shout.

Pam clapped her hand over Anna's mouth with a *Sh-sh*.

Lulu quickly opened the front door. Now Snow White didn't want to leave the house. She was looking all over for Alfie.

Anna let her sniff Alfie's new travel box and went through the door with it. Snow White followed.

The girls and Alfie led her back to the paddock.

"It's two in the morning," Pam announced as they were going back to the house. "Let's try to get some sleep."

"First we have to put everything away in the kitchen," said Lulu.

"And empty that pail," said Pam.

"What pail?" asked Anna.

"Snow White did her business in the house," Lulu explained to Anna. "Pam caught it in a pail."

Anna wrinkled her nose. "I'm glad that wasn't my job," she giggled.

Pam and Anna straightened up the kitchen and put the dry goods back in the cupboard. Lulu emptied the pail of pony plop.

Finally, it was time for the sleep part of the Pony Pals' sleepover. The girls were exhausted. Alfie, on the other hand, was very awake. He played with his papers, nibbled his food, and tipped over his water. He also tried to walk upside down on the strainer roof of his temporary home.

It took Lulu a long time to fall asleep. A knock on the bedroom door woke her a few hours later.

"What?" she called in a sleepy voice.

The door opened. It was Grandmother. "Lucinda, did you find that rodent?" she asked.

"Yes," answered Lulu sleepily. She pointed to the cookie tin. "He's in there."

Grandmother backed up a few steps. "I'll cancel the exterminator then," she said.

Anna and Pam were awake now, too.

The phone rang.

"I thought the phone was broken," said Pam.

"There was a dial tone this morning," explained Grandmother. "The problem must have been outside the house."

Lulu jumped up and gave her grandmother a hug. "Morning, Grandma," she said. "Isn't it a beautiful day?"

Alfie scratched on the roof of his new travel container.

Grandmother looked suspiciously at the hamster tin. "It will be a beautiful day when that creature is out of here," she said.

After breakfast, the Pony Pals and Alfie

waited on the front porch for Rosalie and Mike. Pam and Anna sat on the porch swing. Lulu sat on the porch railing. They were only there a minute when Grandmother Sanders came out.

"I found something strange on the kitchen floor," she said.

"What?" asked Lulu.

Grandmother held up a few strands of stiff white hair. Lulu gulped. Grandmother had found hair from Snow White's mane.

"It's very thick and stiff," said Grandmother. She looked confused. "I know a lot about hair. And I can tell you this is not human hair."

"I know what it is," said Anna.

"You do?" said Lulu.

"It's from Snow White's mane," Anna blurted out.

Pam and Lulu looked at each other with alarm. Lulu's heart sank. Why did Anna tell Grandmother that?

"Why would Snow White's hair be in my kitchen?" asked Grandmother.

"It's simple," answered Anna cheerfully. She turned to Lulu. "Remember when we brushed out the ponies yesterday, Lulu?"

Lulu nodded.

"I bet hair from Snow White's mane was on your clothes," continued Anna. "It fell off in the kitchen."

"Really, Lucinda," said her grandmother. "You must be more careful."

Grandmother dropped the white hairs onto the front lawn and went back inside.

Lulu almost burst from trying not to laugh.

Pam covered her mouth to hold her laughter in.

Anna grinned. "Quick thinking, huh?" she said.

"Except that you almost gave me a heart attack." Lulu giggled.

"There's Rosalie," said Pam, pointing across the Town Green.

Rosalie was running ahead of Mike.

"We found him," Lulu and Anna called out.

Mike caught up with Rosalie and they crossed Main Street together.

Lulu took Alfie out of his box and held him out for Rosalie. She kissed, hugged, and petted him. "Alfie. I'm sorry. I'm sorry, Alfie," she murmured again and again.

Lulu thought Rosalie sounded sad.

Anna put a hand on Rosalie's shoulder. "He's safe now," she said. "You should be happy."

Rosalie gave Alfie to Anna. Tears streamed down her face. "Here," she said. "I can't keep him. Will you take care of him, Anna?"

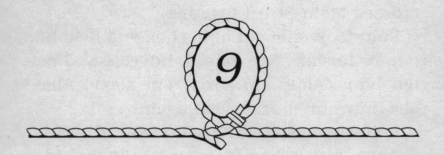

Nobody's Fault

"Did your mother say you can't keep Alfie?" Anna asked Rosalie.

Rosalie shook her head no.

Mike squatted in front of her. "Don't you want him anymore?"

Rosalie nodded her head yes. "But I can't keep him," she mumbled. "I can't."

"Why not?" asked Pam.

"Because I don't take good care of pets," answered Rosalie. "I lost Alfie *three* times and . . . and . . . and I almost *killed* Acorn."

"You didn't almost kill Acorn," said Anna.

"Sometimes ponies can die of tummy aches," explained Rosalie. "You said."

"But Acorn wasn't very sick yesterday, Rosalie," said Anna. "Don't worry about that anymore. Okay?"

"Okay," mumbled Rosalie.

Mike leaned on the porch railing. Rosalie leaned against his leg. Alfie was back in his container on Anna's lap.

No one said anything for at least a minute.

Finally, Lulu broke the silence.

"Once, when Snow White was sick," she began, "she stayed at the Baxters'."

"She couldn't stay with Acorn because she had something that was catching," explained Anna.

"I knew Snow White was lonely at the Baxters'," continued Lulu. "But I was tired, so I went home." Lulu leaned closer to Rosalie. "That night, Snow White ran away and fell in an icy hole. It was my fault. I thought I couldn't keep Snow White after that."

Anna smiled at Lulu. "But we convinced you to keep her."

"Do you think Lulu should have given up her pony?" Pam asked Rosalie

"No," answered Rosalie softly.

"I had my first pets when I was your age, Rosalie," said Anna. "Three goldfish in a bowl. My mother said I was giving them too much to eat."

"Like I gave Acorn too many treats?" asked Rosalie.

"Yes," agreed Anna. "Except the goldfish didn't do tricks. Anyway, I liked to feed the goldfish. So I did."

"Even though her mother said not to," said Pam.

Anna nodded. "And they died because I fed them too much," concluded Anna.

"All of them?" asked Rosalie.

Anna nodded. "Goldilocks, Mother Goose, and Humpty Dumpty," she said sadly. "It was my fault."

Rosalie went over to the swing and squeezed in between Pam and Anna. She patted Anna on the arm. "That's okay," she

said. "Don't be sad." She turned to Pam. "Did you ever hurt an animal?"

Pam pushed the floor with her foot. The porch swing moved back and forth.

"I yelled at my dog, Woolie," remembered Pam. "And he ran away."

"What happened?" asked Rosalie with alarm.

"He got hurt in the woods," said Pam. "And it was my fault."

"I lost Alfie three times," said Rosalie.

"But he didn't get injured," said Pam.

"Or sick," added Anna. She put Alfie's container on Rosalie's lap.

"I just thought of something else," said Lulu.

"What?" asked Rosalie.

"I left you alone and you ran away," she said. "That was my fault."

"I didn't run away," said Rosalie. "I went for a ride."

Lulu tickled Rosalie until she begged for mercy.

"Will you keep Alfie now?" Mike asked his sister.

Rosalie looked down at her sleeping hamster. "What if he runs away again?" she asked.

"He wouldn't get away if you didn't walk around with him all the time," said Mike.

"He doesn't like to be alone," said Rosalie. "He gets bored." She looked down at her hamster. "Don't you, Alfie?"

"What's his house like?" asked Lulu.

"It's a cage with food and water," answered Mike.

"He has a wheel, too," added Rosalie. "But it's broken."

"Hamsters need tunnels and wheels that work," said Lulu. "They get bored easily."

Anna jumped up. "Let's fix up his cage," she suggested.

Rosalie looked around at the four older kids. "Can we all do it together?" she asked.

"Sure," agreed Lulu and Pam.

"Let's go to my place to do it," suggested Anna. "We can work at the picnic table."

"I'll go get the cage," offered Mike.

Half an hour later, the Pony Pals, Mike, and Rosalie had agreed on a design for Alfie's cage.

ALFIE'S HOUSE

MATERIALS
From Anna's Dollhouse
Ladder
Garage
From the Beauty parlor
Plastic curlers
Bobby pins
Clips
Old newspaper

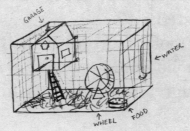

Anna went to her room to get the doll-house parts. Lulu went to the beauty parlor for the rollers and bobby pins. When they came back, everyone went to work.

Mike and Pam fixed the wheel with bobby pins.

Rosalie shredded up paper for the floor of the cage.

Lulu took the door off the dollhouse garage. She held the little garage halfway up one inside wall of the cage. Anna clipped it in place.

Anna leaned the ladder against the open side of the garage. Lulu clipped that in place, too.

Mike twirled the wheel. "We fixed it," he said proudly.

"Uh-oh," Anna whispered to Lulu. She was looking toward the driveway.

Lulu turned and saw Tommy barrel down the driveway on his bike. Mike saw him, too. His expression turned from happy to worried.

Home-Sweet-Home

Tommy came at full speed right up to the table. Pam quickly pulled in her legs. Tommy slid his bike wheels to a stop where Pam's legs had been.

"Hey!" exclaimed Pam.

"Tommy, we're fixing up a house for my hamster," said Rosalie cheerfully.

Tommy laughed loudly. It was a laugh that made fun of other people. "Is Mikey making a house for the little itty-bitty hamster?" he asked.

Mike put down the pink plastic wheel and looked at the table.

Tommy slapped Mike on the back. "Come on, man. Let's go fishing," he said.

Lulu and Anna exchanged a glance. What would Mike do?

"I can't go fishing today," said Mike softly. "I'm watching Rosalie."

"There are three *girls* to watch Rosalie," said Tommy.

Mike looked up. "She's my responsibility," he said. "It's my job."

"Alfie's so cute, Tommy," said Rosalie. She held Alfie right up to Tommy's face. He jumped back, tripped over his own bike, and landed on his backside.

"Tommy's afraid of the little itty-bitty hamster," teased Anna.

Mike put out his hand to help Tommy up.

"I am not," said Tommy.

"He isn't," insisted Mike. "Rosalie just surprised him." He turned to his sister. "Put Alfie away or you'll lose him again."

Tommy righted his bike. "I've got better things to do than hang around here," he said. And he left as quickly as he came.

"Tommy's silly sometimes," said Rosalie.

"He sure is," mumbled Mike. "Come on, let's finish this thing."

Rosalie put in the clean, shredded paper.

Mike put in the wheel.

Pam clipped on a water bottle and put down a dish of food.

Finally, the new hamster house was perfect.

"Can Alfie go in it now?" asked Rosalie.

"That's the idea," said Mike. "Let's see how he likes it."

Rosalie carefully put Alfie in the center of the cage. First, he ran around the first floor. Next, he tried his wheel. His little legs moved quickly as it spun. He jumped out of the wheel and looked around. He saw the ladder and scurried over to it. Up he climbed to the dollhouse garage. He walked to the middle of the garage floor and sat down.

The Pony Pals, Mike, and Rosalie were watching his every move.

"What do we have here?" a male voice asked. Lulu turned and saw her father standing behind her.

"Dad!" she shrieked. Lulu jumped up and gave her father a big hug.

"Hi, honey," he said.

"I thought you were in Africa. I thought I wouldn't see you for so long," Lulu said in a rush. "But you're *here!*"

"We finished early. I have two weeks before I go to India." He smiled down at her. "So I came home."

Mr. Harley put an arm around his daughter's shoulder and looked around at her friends. "Hi, guys," he said.

Rosalie held Alfie up for him to see. Mr. Sanders admired the small animal and his cage.

They all took turns telling Mr. Sanders about the adventures of the missing hamster.

"And Snow White's the one who found him," concluded Anna.

"Two times," added Rosalie.

Mr. Sanders laughed heartily. "Imagine if

my mother saw a pony in her kitchen," he said. "I wouldn't want to be around for that."

He looked toward the paddock. Snow White was standing at the fence watching all the activity.

"I haven't said hello to Snow White," he said.

Lulu and her father walked hand in hand to the paddock.

Mr. Sanders patted Snow White's muzzle. "Hi, Snow White," he said. "You took good care of Lulu while I was gone. Thanks."

Snow White nickered as if to say, "You're welcome."

"I'm really proud of her," said Lulu. She put her arm around Snow White's neck and kissed her cheek. "I love Snow White so much, Dad."

Lulu's father kissed the top of Lulu's head. "I love *you*," he said.

Lulu felt a lump form in her throat. She swallowed the tears of happiness and looked up at her father and smiled. "I'm glad you're home, Dad."

Dear Reader,

I am having fun researching and writing the Pony Pal books. I've met great kids and wonderful ponies at homes, farms, and riding schools. Some of my ideas for Pony Pal adventures have even come from these visits.

I remember the day I made up the main characters for the series. I was walking on a country road in New England. First, I decided that the three girls would be smart, independent, and kind. Then I gave them their names—Pam, Anna, and Lulu. (Look at the initial of each girl's name. See what it spells when you put them together.) Later, I created the three ponies. When I reached home, I turned on my computer and started to write. And I haven't stopped since!

My friends say that I am a little bit like all of the Pony Pals. I am very organized, like Pam. I love nature, like Lulu. But I think that I am most like Anna. I am dyslexic and a good artist, just like her.

Many Pony Pal readers send me letters, drawings, and photos. I tape them to the wall in my office. They inspire me to write more Pony Pal stories. Thank you very much!

I don't ride anymore and I've never had a pony. But you don't have to ride to love ponies! And you certainly don't need a pony to be a Pony Pal.

Happy Reading, *Jeanne Betancourt*

P.S.
Rosalie Lacey appears in many Pony Pal stories. Look for her in #5: PONY TO THE RESCUE, #14: PONY-SITTERS, #21: THE WINNING PONY, #29: LOST AND FOUND PONY.

In chapter nine of this story, the Pony Pals tell Rosalie about mistakes they've made with animals. Snow White ran away in #7: THE RUNAWAY PONY. Pam's dog Woolie ran away in #27: THE PONY AND THE MISSING DOG. Anna overfed her fish before she was a Pony Pal.